Tiny Fox and Great Boar

Furthest

Berenika Kołomycka

Tiny Fox and Great Boar

Furthest

Written and Illustrated by Berenika Kołomycka
Lettered by Crank!

AN ONI PRESS PUBLICATION

Designed by Kate Z. Stone
Edited by Grace Scheipeter

Published by Oni-Lion Forge Publishing Group, LLC.

James Lucas Jones, president & publisher • Charlie Chu, e.v.p. of creative & business development • Steve Ellis, e.v.p. of games & operations • Alex Segura, s.v.p of marketing & sales • Michelle Nguyen, associate publisher • Brad Rooks, director of operations • Katie Sainz, director of marketing • Tara Lehmann, publicity director • Henry Barajas, sales manager • Holly Aitchison, consumer marketing manager • Lydia Nguyen, marketing intern Troy Look, director of design & production • Angie Knowles, production manager • Carey Hall, graphic designer • Sarah Rockwell, graphic designer • Hilary Thompson, graphic designer • Vincent Kukua, digital prepress technician • Chris Cerasi, managing editor Jasmine Amiri, senior editor • Amanda Meadows, senior editor • Bess Pallares, editor Desiree Rodriguez, editor • Grace Scheipeter, editor • Zack Soto, editor • Gabriel Granillo, editorial assistant • Ben Eisner, game developer • Sara Harding, entertainment executive assistant • Jung Lee, logistics coordinator • Kuian Kellum, warehouse assistant

Joe Nozemack, publisher emeritus

1319 SE Martin Luther King Jr. Blvd.
Suite 240
Portland, OR 97214

onipress.com
🅵 🅥 🅘 @onipress

@berenikamess
@ccrank

First Edition: November 2022
ISBN: 978-1-63715-092-4
eISBN: 978-1-63715-112-9

1 2 3 4 5 6 7 8 9 10

Library of Congress Control Number: 2022932797

Printed in China

Far

After many great adventures, Tiny Fox and Great Boar left the forest behind.

Everything around them seemed different, but the friends were not afraid, because they were together.

They walked happily.

They had no worries.

They were bursting
with energy.

Tiny Fox and Great Boar were enjoying the beautiful weather...

...the meadow, and each other.

They enjoyed every day.

10

11

They were lying and thinking of the wind, which blows over here, then over there...
...and of all the smells that come with it.
Boar, look at the clouds. They are delightful.
Hmm... yes...

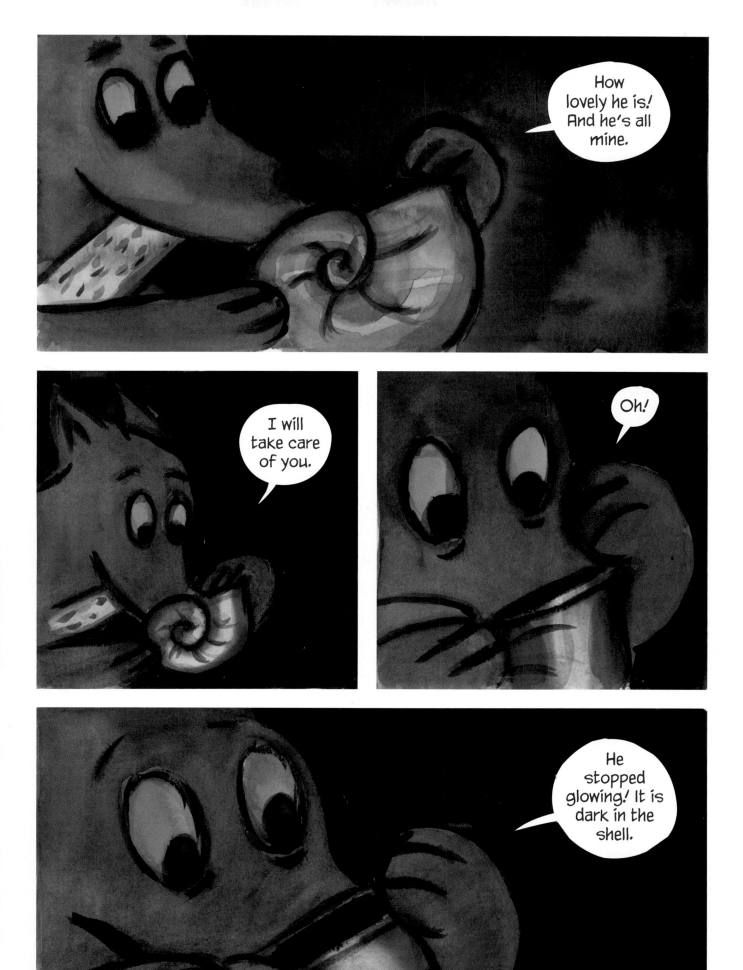

Further

The meadow
was wonderful.

The animals' days were
passing without a care.
They had everything
they needed.

Every day the
sky was blue.

The grass smelled lovely,
and in the evenings, fireflies
came to light up the dark.

Everything slowly lost color.

How miserable it is here.

And gray.

There was complete silence. Even the sounds of their walking were lost in the fog.

And if we vanish too?

Will we be gone forever?

Brrr!

I would never see you again, nor you me.

How horrible...

The fog was getting thicker and thicker.

Now a firefly would be useful.

Fox, I don't think fireflies would glow here. They are shyer than us.

The animals felt
very lonely.

It felt like all their hopes
and dreams disappeared
in the thick fog.

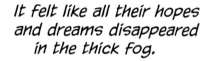

Fox,
I think I'll
stay here. I am
already invisible
anyway.

I'm
getting
tired.

34

Furthest

49

Boar, you know you won't turn into a seal.

You have hooves, and I have claws so that we can walk on the ground.

Seals will never see our apple tree or the mountain tops.

They won't lie on soft grass or enjoy a rainbow above a valley.

Fox, I forgot about you.

I'm sorry.

55

An early sketch of page nine from this book.
Tiny Fox and Great Boar are bursting with energy!

Some paintings of a few flowers and plants that Tiny Fox
and Great Boar encountered on their journey. Can you find
any of these flowers and plants in the book?

More sketches of flowers and plants.
Do you like to explore nature?

Another early sketch that inspired this book.
Can you find the butterfly? Try to paint one yourself!

Tiny Fox and Great Boar happily
embarking on a new adventure!

Berenika Kołomycka

Berenika Kołomycka is a comics author, sketch artist, sculptor, and graphic artist. She graduated from the Academy of Fine Arts in Warsaw and earned the Grand Prix for comics at the International Festival of Comics and Games in Łódź. Her works have been published in both Polish and foreign magazines, as well as in schoolbooks. She regularly conducts comic workshops for adults and children. The children's comic book series *Tiny Fox and Great Boar* is her first solo project. Outside of her work, she enjoys taking care of her cat, Mami, and her dog, Kuka.

Crank!

Christopher Crank (crank!) has lettered a bunch of books put out by Image, Dark Horse, Oni Press, Dynamite, and elsewhere. He also has a podcast with comic artist Mike Norton and members of Four Star Studios in Chicago (crankcast.com), and makes music (sonomorti.bandcamp.com). Catch him on Twitter: @ccrank and Instagram: ccrank